A Pet
Called Persil

Viv Sayer

Illustrated by
Petra Brown

PONT READALONE

Published in 2006 by Pont Books, an imprint of
Gomer Press, Llandysul, Ceredigion SA44 4JL

ISBN 1 84323 649 4
ISBN-13 9781843236498
A CIP record for this title is available from the British Library

This book is published with the financial support of the
Welsh Books Council.

Printed and bound in Wales at
Gomer Press, Llandysul, Ceredigion SA44 4JL

In memory of my dad,
storyteller extraordinary

Chapter 1

Madi's Secret

'Izzy, you'll never guess!' Madlen hurled her book bag onto the table, then peeled off her coat and flung it over the back of the chair. She rewound her scarf, making a double dayglo loop around her neck.

'What?' I said.

Madlen twiddled the ends of her scarf. She loves secrets, so I knew I was in for a long wait.

At that moment our teacher, Mrs Thomas, came into the classroom. 'There's a special prize for anyone who can find me the music for *Seren Nadolig.*' She looked at Sara hopefully.

'Mrs Thomas! Not again!' scolded Sara. 'I found it the last time.' I wouldn't dare say something like that to Mrs T, but it was okay. She was busy rummaging through the papers on her desk.

'What's the prize?' asked Aled. He laid his trumpet case carefully under the worktop where the computers sat.

'If you found my music for me, you'd find out, wouldn't you!' Mrs Thomas looked up and smiled suddenly. It can't have been that urgent then. It would turn up; things usually did.

'Right. Sara! Aled! Isabel! Madlen! Out you go! Fresh air in the yard till the bell goes.'

Madi and I took our time in the classroom in the mornings, hoping Mrs Thomas would send us on errands so that we didn't have to go outside and risk being struck by a flying football. Richard knew he wasn't supposed to kick the ball outside the pitch, but he got a real buzz out of aiming at people's heads, especially girls'.

'Out you go!'

Madi tried a delaying tactic. 'Where do I put this?' she said, waving a long brown envelope.

'What is it?'

'Dinner money.'

'Usual place, Madlen.' Mrs Thomas wasn't going to give in. 'Now out you go, the pair of you! And put your coats on. It's cold.'

When we got outside, Ffion had taken a direct hit from a football and was sitting on the bench holding the side of her face. Madlen put her arm around her.

'I know what it's like,' she said. 'He did it to

me last week. It'll sting for a bit, but you'll be all right.'

Ffion dabbed at her eyes and tried to smile. I expect she was remembering what Madlen had been like after her 'accident' with Richard and his football. She had cried non-stop until after Assembly.

'And anyway,' continued Madlen, 'I've got some really cool news.'

At that moment the bell rang. In the cloakroom I hung up my coat quickly and waited while Madi fussed with her PE bag.

'Come on, Madi,' I said after a bit. 'What's the big secret?'

Madlen spun around. 'I'm going to have a dog.'

'What? Your mum has said you can have one of the puppies?' Fly, our sheepdog, had a litter about a month ago.

'Is it okay?' Madi was serious for a moment. 'I mean after . . .'

When the puppies were born, one of them was smaller than the others and didn't know how to feed. Mum fed her from a bottle and she got a bit stronger, but it was no good. One morning Mum woke me up and said I had to be brave because the smallest of the puppies had died in the night. Alys and Rhodri were really upset, but I was saddest because it is my job to look after Fly.

'No, it's all right,' I said. 'Come on. We're going to be late.'

I was really happy. Madi and I have been friends ever since we started together in the *meithrin* and in all that time she's never been allowed to have a dog. Her brother gets asthma really badly – I mean, he gets so bad sometimes that he has to go to hospital.

Mrs Thomas had only just started the dinner register. She has to do three different registers in the morning and gets really ratty if anybody interrupts her.

'There's someone at the door,' shouted Steffan.

Mrs Thomas looked up crossly. It was Angharad from Year 6 with a note from Mr Morris. 'Concert practice at ten o'clock,' Mrs Thomas read out. 'Well, Blwyddyn 5, at this rate we're never going to finish fractions!'

When we were lining up to go into the hall, Madlen somehow managed to beat the system – we're supposed to stand in alphabetical order – and came to stand next to me.

'Isabel?'

'Mm.'

'D'you think Friday would be okay for me to come over and see the puppies?'

Mum is always pleased when my friends came to the farm. We live a long way out of town and, because we're the only Welsh school for miles, everyone gets bussed in from different places. 'Course,' I said. 'Dad'll take you home after milking.'

'No, it's okay,' said Madlen. 'It'll work better if Mum picks me up.'

I should have known she was planning something, but at that moment Mrs Collins had started calling the actors into the hall. Madi was playing the part of the Angel Gabriel and, as usual, she had left her harp in the classroom.

Chapter 2

Pero

I like Fridays. It's the best day of the week – fish and chips for dinner, and then games in the afternoon. And this Friday was even better: Madi was coming home on the bus with me to choose one of the puppies.

After school, all the bus people go down to the hall, where each bus line has its own special place. Families always sit together. Today Jonathan, Madi's brother, had to go home without her, so she went over to talk to him before coming to sit with us. My sister, Alys, couldn't wait to show Madi her picture. She'd painted it in Golden Time and it was supposed to be Fly and the puppies. Madi had to say which puppy she liked best. They all looked the same to me – black blobs with patches of white and streaks for legs. Madlen was really tactful and said they were all lovely.

Our bus was the last to arrive – as usual – but Mr Morris was on duty and made up a quiz to pass the time. He's quite funny – for a teacher.

The little ones got questions like, 'If I have five buns and I eat one, will I still be hungry?' He asked Dafydd to guess what Mrs Thomas was going to have for supper and Dafydd thought it was a real question! The jokes had started to wear a bit thin, though, by the time our bus finally came – there had been a big hold-up on the bridge because of the road works. Our driver, Bryn, is really nice, not like the man on the Llynygraig bus – but I expect he's grouchy because he has to take Richard to school every day.

When we reached the farm gate, I could see Mum's car parked up behind the barn. She comes home early on Fridays, and there was a warm smell of baking as I pushed open the kitchen door.

'Hi, girls! Hi, Rhodri!'

Mum sent us all to wash our hands ready for tea, but I just had to take Madi to see the puppies first. Their basket is in the old dairy so we poked our noses around the door to see what they were doing. The three of them were cuddled up to Fly. Her tail wagged but no way was she going to leave her babies to come and say hello.

'They're gorgeous,' Madlen sighed.

'Which one do you like the best? They'll be ready to leave Fly in about a fortnight.'

'I don't know. The one with the patch on his ear is cute.'

I knew she'd like Pero. He was my favourite too.

It was after eight o'clock and already dark when we heard a knock at the back door. Madlen's mum looked tired after her evening class at the High School and sat down gratefully at the kitchen table while Mum made her a cup of coffee. I couldn't work out why Madi wasn't pestering her mother to go and see the puppies straight away. It wasn't like her at all. Once we were out in the passage, I asked her what was going on.

Madlen looked past me towards the dairy.

'They haven't said "yes", have they?' I said. Suddenly I knew what she was up to. 'You won't get away with it.'

'I will. Just watch me.'

Madlen stood in the kitchen doorway, cradling Pero in her arms like a baby.

'Oh, *cariad.*' Madi's mum was up from the table. 'Be careful with him.'

The next half hour was really horrible. I hate being around when other people are having a row. And that's what it turned into when Madlen's mum realised she had been set up. Madi had banked on looking so cute holding the puppy that her mum just wouldn't be able to say no.

'*Cariad*, you know we can't have a dog. Think about Jonathan. He's only got to see one and he starts wheezing.'

'Please, Mum. I'll keep him away from Jonathan. I'll take him for walks. You won't even know he's in the house.'

My mum raised her eyebrows but said nothing. Madlen started to cry – not wailing or anything,

just wet eyes and a quiet snuffle. The puppy licked her face.

'Come and sit with me.' Madlen's mum led her to the sofa and put her arm around her. 'I'd like to say "yes". I really would. We always had a dog when I was a little girl, but I didn't have a brother with a bad chest.'

Madi didn't say anything. She leaned her cheek against Pero's velvety ear and hot tears splashed onto his coat. Mum had quietly taken Rhodri and Alys off to the bathroom. It was way past their bedtime. I didn't know what to do. I couldn't just walk away, but I didn't want to be part of it either. At last Madi's mum spoke.

'Okay. I'll do a deal.'

Madi looked up hopefully.

'You've been cuddling Fly and the puppies for hours. When we go home tonight, we won't tell Jonathan. We'll see how his asthma is over the weekend. If he's still okay on Sunday night, I promise I'll give the dog idea some serious thought.'

It was like sunshine after rain. Madlen tried to give her mum a hug but forgot all about Pero. He gave a sharp little yap and wriggled down off the sofa. He had had enough.

Chapter 3

A Brave Face

I couldn't wait to get to school on Monday; it was going to be great, making a list with Madi of all the things she would need for Pero. It was raining heavily that morning. Because it was too wet to play outside, we were allowed to stay in the classroom. Alun came in, got his book out and sat down to read. He only does it so that Mrs Thomas will say what a good boy he is. Dyfed had brought in a set of rocks and was putting them out on the big display table.

I was on my way over to have a look when I saw Madlen at the classroom door. She looked awful; her eyes were red and her face was all blotchy as if she'd been crying for weeks. Her mum was talking to Mrs Thomas, who was nodding and looking sympathetic.

When I went up to her, Madi waved me away and shook her head. She didn't want to talk.

We don't have school assembly on a Monday. We have Circle Time in our classroom instead.

Usually Mrs Thomas tells us a story or reads us something from the newspaper. Then we have a discussion about it. We can say anything we like, so long as it doesn't hurt anybody's feelings.

I managed to sit next to Madlen but she just kept twisting a tissue between her fingers and wouldn't look at me. Mrs Thomas read us a bit from *The Diary of Anne Frank* and afterwards she asked us what we thought being brave really meant.

Aled wasn't sure whether Anne Frank was brave or not. 'It's braver if you choose to do something really hard,' he said. It's awful, what happened to Anne Frank, but she didn't have a choice. She had to stay hidden, didn't she?'

'What about Gethin? He didn't have a choice.' Steffan's younger brother had to have an operation to help him walk properly and had to be in a wheelchair for the whole of last year. 'He was ever so brave. He didn't cry, even when his legs were really hurting.'

That was it. Everybody had something to say – Sara whose brother fell out of the treehouse and broke his arm, and Gemma whose mum scalded herself and had to go to hospital. After a while, Mrs Thomas held up her hand.

'Well done, Blwyddyn 5,' she said, 'You listened to each other really well. There's just one thing I'd like to add. I'm not going to name any names, but I heard this morning about somebody who had to make a very courageous decision over the weekend.' Everybody looked around. Madi was staring miserably into her lap. I took her hand and squeezed it.

At playtime I caught up with her on her way to the shelter. It was still raining, but the infants can always go out to play because there's a long porch that runs right along their side of the building. Because we like helping the little ones, we get to spend one playtime a week in their playground. Already Carys was pulling at Madlen's coat. '*Ga i ganu'r gloch?*' she said. That's all they want to do, the infants – ring the bell for the end of playtime. You'd think they like being cooped up in their classroom all day.

'Mrs Thomas was talking about you, wasn't she?'

Madlen nodded.

'What happened?'

'When we got home on Friday, Jonathan ran straight up to me and gave me a big hug. He never does that normally. I suppose it was because me and Mum were late home. He was okay at first, but at bedtime he started to cough, and then he just got worse and worse. I couldn't sleep because I could hear Mum and Dad in his room. He was coughing and coughing. Then he started to make that horrible noise, the one he makes when he's really bad. It's like he's sucking in air. When I went in to see, Dad was just wrapping him up in a blanket. Mum had called the ambulance because she knew Jonathan needed to go to hospital.'

'What happened then?'

'It was ages before the ambulance arrived.

18

Then it came and Mum and I went to the window to see them go. I cried for a bit – but Mum gave me a cuddle and said that everything was going to be fine. Once Jonathan had had the nebuliser stuff, he would be okay.'

'What's nebu whatsit?'

'Stuff to help him breathe. It comes out of a machine – he has to wear a mask.'

'Poor thing,' I said.

Madi gulped. 'Then I asked was it because of the puppies and Mum said we couldn't be sure but it was a bit of a coincidence and I said I'd never ask for a dog ever again, if Jonathan could be all right.' She stopped for breath. 'I went to sleep then, and in the morning when I woke up, Jonathan was back home.'

'But you'd already said you'd give up the puppy idea.'

'Yeah. And I was okay about it, I really was, till last night. Then I started thinking about having to tell you that I couldn't have Pero.' She was really crying now and Mrs Rees, the teacher on duty, had started walking towards us.

'Come on,' I said. 'Let's ask if we can empty the fruit into the compost bin.' I needed time to think.

Chapter 4

The School Council

I had a plan. I just had to choose the right moment, even if it took till Circle Time the following week. But then I had a stroke of luck – a message came round to say that there would be a school council meeting on Thursday lunchtime. The school council is new. We've had an eco-committee for ages – that's where we decide how we are going to help the environment, like turning off lights and recycling paper. We had to vote for class representatives for the eco-committee, then we had to have another vote for the school council. Edward Davies and I were chosen as the school councillors for Blwyddyn 5.

Just before hometime on Wednesday, Mrs Thomas sent us to sit on the carpet to talk about Thursday's meeting. Ffion wanted us to ask about having safe areas in the playground for people who didn't want to play football. Eleri complained that someone kept moving her bag in the cloakroom. This usually means that she has forgotten where she put her things. I said I'd ask if other people's bags were being moved. Nobody could think of anything else. I was careful not to look at Madlen – and took a deep breath. 'I've got something,' I said. 'I think we should ask if we can have a class pet.'

'A pet?' Aled sounded scornful. 'What for?'

I ignored him. 'In my cousin's school, every class has its own pet. They've got gerbils, Siôn and Siân.'

'What else have they got?'

'Man-eating snakes.' Steffan hissed and draped his hands over his neighbour's shoulder like a pair of fangs.

'Don't be silly, Steffan.' Mrs Thomas is supposed to keep out of it when we are talking, but she just can't help butting in. Next she wanted to ask a question.

'In your cousin's school, who looks after the pets, feeds them, cleans them out and so on?'

'They take turns. The teachers don't have to do anything,' I said quickly in case she decided that it was too much hard work.

'What happens at the weekends and in the holidays?'

'Weekends are okay. People take the gerbils home. And in the holidays.'

I looked over at Madlen. She was staring out of the window.

I couldn't believe how easy it was at the school council meeting. I think it must have been on the teachers' secret list of things-to-do-to-make-the-school-a-better-place. When it was our turn, I got straight to the point.

'Some people in our class can't able have an animal at home, and we thought it would be nice if they could get to look after one in school. We'd like a class pet.'

Mrs Hughes couldn't have looked more pleased if I had said we had won first prize in the Urdd Eisteddfod. 'Isabel,' she said, 'that is a really excellent idea. The school council is all about learning about how to look after others, and I can't think of a better way of doing that than taking care of an animal.'

Mr Morris laughed at this point and Mrs Hughes gave him a look. 'Of course,' she said, 'I will have to discuss this carefully with the other teachers and I'll let you know as soon as I can.'

It was as easy as that. During last play on

Friday, Mrs Hughes sent for me and Edward, and said that the teachers had agreed. And they had also decided that our class should try out the idea first. If everybody adopted an animal, Mrs Hughes said, the school would look like Noah's ark!

It meant a new round of voting, because everybody had different ideas about the best kind of animal for our class. In theory, we could have an indoor or an outdoor pet – there was plenty of room outside for a run and a hutch, but, as Ffion said, flying footballs wouldn't be very good for rabbits or guinea pigs either and she wouldn't put anything past Richard.

Of course, the boys just had to go over the top. Steffan wanted something dramatic, like a tarantula, the bigger the better. The girls wanted something that could be picked up and stroked. Steffan said that tarantulas could be stroked. In the end, the vote was between gerbils and hamsters. We went onto the internet for information. I voted for hamsters because the gerbils looked too much like rats to me: we get plenty of rats on the farm and I just hate their whippy tails.

Madlen was so lucky. When we drew straws out of a hat to see who was going to go with Mrs Thomas to look at the hamsters down at the

garden centre the following Monday lunchtime, hers was the longest by a mile.

'Aren't you pleased?' I'd sneaked across to Madlen's bus queue.

'Yes.' She didn't sound too sure.

'What's wrong?'

'It's not the same as a dog, is it?'

'Well, no. But it's better than nothing.'

'S'pose. What if I smell of hamster when I get home?'

At that moment Mrs Collins called Madlen's bus.

Chapter 5

Hamster Poo

Madi was a lot more upbeat on Monday after going to the garden centre. They had taken the digital camera with them and she couldn't wait to print out the pictures and tell everybody about the hamsters they'd seen and the different cages.

'There's this brilliant one with towers and tunnels. It's like the kind of thing hamsters would build in the wild. And we can buy extra bits if we want to make the cage bigger.'

'Hamster mansions,' said Edward, when Madi showed us the picture. Everybody laughed.

'What about the hamster?' asked Ffion. 'No point in having a cage without a hamster.'

Madlen spread the pictures out on the carpet. Immediately the boys surged forward, blocking everyone else's view. Mrs Thomas ordered them back and said the best thing would be to put the pictures on the noticeboard and put a number against each one so that everybody could see them. And then everyone could have a piece of paper . . .

'Not another vote,' groaned Steff.

'It's the fairest way,' said Mrs Thomas. And everybody agreed.

'I, the returning officer,' said Mrs T, 'do hereby declare that hamster number,' she paused, 'four . . . has been duly elected to represent this classroom.'

'Why's she saying that?' whispered Sara.

'That's how they do it on the telly in a real election,' said Aled. 'I expect we'll have to vote for its name as well.'

That turned out to be unnecessary. The minute he set eyes on the snowy bundle of fur in its travelling cage, Morgan shouted out, 'Persil!'

'Persil?' said Mrs Thomas.

'Yes,' he said, 'whiter than white!' And the name stuck.

For the next few weeks, the first thing anybody in our class did when they got to school was rush into class to see Persil. He was so cute and really tame. Mum said it was because so many different people handled him. He quickly got used to being taken out of his cage, and would run from one hand to the other of whoever was holding him.

Mrs Thomas wasn't very happy when he was out of the cage so he was only ever allowed out for a few minutes at a time. I think she was worried, even then, that he might escape.

Edward and I had to draw up a rota of who was going to clean the cage each week, and who was going to change Persil's food and water. Mrs Thomas said she would get his bedding and stuff. At first she bought wood shavings, but at an eco-committee meeting they decided that we should use recycled shredded paper.

The first time Hamster Mansions was cleaned, Sara and Edward were in charge, but Mrs T let everybody watch so that we would all know what to do when it was our turn. At first we couldn't work out where Persil was going to go when we mucked out the middle part of the cage – his main living area.

'I know,' said Sara at last. 'If we can get Persil to go up in his tower, I can lift it off and keep my hand under the tube to stop him coming out.' From Persil's living area, plastic tubes ran up to a smaller tower room.

'Right!' said Edward. 'But how are you going to get him up there?'

'Easy,' said Sara. 'If we put some food in the tower, he'll come zooming up to see what's there.' This was true. Even when Persil was asleep – and hamsters are supposed to sleep during the day – he only had to hear the rattle of plastic, then he would poke his nose out from his nest and shoot up the tube to see what had landed in his feeding bowl. He was so funny when he ate. He just stuffed and stuffed until all the food was gone and his cheeks stuck out like panniers – that's what Mrs Thomas called them.

Sara's plan worked. Just as she said, Persil shot up into the tower and she found it quite easy to work the tube loose and slide it out of the lower chamber. She held the tower room – plus Persil –

in one hand and covered the lower end of the tube with the other. It was then that she made her big discovery.

'He's been nibbling the plastic,' she said. 'The end of this tube is all rough.'

'The man in the garden centre said that only gerbils do that.' Madlen looked over at Mrs Thomas. 'If you have gerbils, you have to buy metal rings to go over the ends of the tubes to stop them being gnawed to bits.'

'Perhaps Persil thinks he's a gerbil.'

While this was going on, Edward had tipped out the old rubbish – bedding, sawdust, hamster poo – onto a sheet of newspaper. 'What a stink!' he said.

'I think we might have to change him more than once a week,' said Mrs Thomas. 'He is a bit whiffy!'

It took quite a long time to wash the cage and put in clean sawdust and bedding. When it was all ready, Sara took her hand out from under the tube and slid it quickly back into the hole in the living room roof.

'I'll go and get those rings after school tonight,' said Mrs Thomas. 'We don't want that hamster eating his way out of his cage.'

It didn't take long to get used to refilling Persil's food dish and water bottle, but cleaning his cage was always a problem.

I never liked it when we had to trick him up into his tower – so I was really pleased when Dyfed brought in a hamster ball – like a see-through plastic football that unscrewed in the middle – so that Persil could travel in it around the room – which must have made a change from just going round and round on the wheel in his cage. The ball was great because he could choose where he went. It was so funny to see his little feet going – he could speed up and slow down and change direction – it was brilliant.

When we did the rota, we teamed up people who didn't have an animal at home with those who did. It worked out well – but I got a surprise when it was our turn, Madi's and mine. Even though there are lots of animals on the farm, I'd never held anything as small as a hamster and I didn't really like the feel of Persil's little paws on my hand. Madlen, though, was really good with him and he was always much calmer when she was holding him, even after a trip in the hamster ball.

Chapter 6

Santes Dwynwen

By the time we broke up for Christmas, most people had had a turn at looking after Persil. He got his own Christmas cards – from girls mainly – and two or three presents. Mrs Thomas opened them on the last day of term and his new toys were installed in his cage. The thing he liked best, we decided, was the hamster mirror. He spent ages looking at it and putting his paw up to touch the glass. Gemma volunteered to take him home for the holidays and, for once, there were no arguments.

He arrived back on the first day of term looking bigger and fluffier than ever and the cleaning rota started all over again.

At the end of January we had a disco to celebrate Santes Dwynwen – she's the Welsh Saint Valentine. On the day before the disco, according to the rota, Stuart and Alex were due to clean Persil's cage.

In the morning we had been doing a science investigation. We had to make up a test to see whether salt or sugar dissolves best in water, and, in the afternoon, we had to write up our findings. Stuart and Alex had already done the practical bit, and Mrs Thomas said they could do the write-up at home to have extra time to change the hamster. They went off to get fresh bedding and sawdust after lunch and came back from the store cupboard with mounds of stuff. They took ages coaxing Persil out of his cage and, by the number of times we heard 'Oh Stuart!', Alex was not impressed by his partner's hamster-handling skills.

I whispered to Madlen, 'If they don't hurry up, they're going to miss games.' Mrs Williams takes us for PE and she doesn't put up with any nonsense. Anyone not in their PE kit by the time she comes over from the infants doesn't get to go out on the field or into the hall.

As it turned out, missing games was going to be the least of their problems.

I guessed that something was wrong when Stuart called Mrs Thomas over to the hamster corner. She was still there when Mrs Parry, the secretary, came up from the office with a message. By this time, Steffan was out of his seat and the rest of us had stopped even pretending to work. We were making a heck of a noise but

Mrs T wasn't taking any notice. Suddenly though, she put her hand up for silence, then said quietly, 'Blwyddyn 5, stop whatever you are doing, put your pens down and listen. We have a problem.'

'Well how did he get out of the ball?' Aled looked accusingly at Stuart. 'You can't have closed it properly. You're useless, you are!'

I could see even from the other side of the room that Stuart was about to cry.

'I did close it properly,' he said. 'He just escaped.'

'Hamsters don't just escape,' said Aled. 'You let him go.'

'That's enough,' said Mrs Thomas. 'This won't get us anywhere. I want everybody to be really, really quiet and have a good look around under the tables. He can't have gone far. Just be very careful about where you are stepping.'

So we all got down on our hands and knees and started to look for Persil at ground level. My desk is near the whiteboard, and there aren't many places for a small animal to hide so I worked my way gradually over to the wet area where there are paint trolleys and lots of drawer units full of paper and printing materials. All the time I was whispering 'here-Persil, here-Persil'.

Suddenly I stopped dead – from under the newspapers down by side of the sink, I thought I could hear rustling. 'Sh!' I whispered as loudly as I dared. 'Sh! I think I've found him!'

I moved very slowly, lying on my tummy on the floor tiles and using my elbows to drag myself forward, trying to make as little sound as possible. Gemma had fetched one of Persil's hamster sandwiches – a snack made out of stuck-together grains and sunflower seeds – and put it into my hand. I couldn't take my eyes off the papers. Every now and again, they twitched, ever so slightly. I could feel everybody's eyes on me, but still I wasn't going to make a move until I was sure he wasn't going to get away.

I couldn't believe what happened next. Steffan must have decided that I was taking too long. He suddenly pushed me out of the way, whisked the newspapers out from under the unit and dived as if he was about to score a try – and the last we saw of Persil was his snowy bottom disappearing into a ventilation pipe.

'You *twpsyn!*' I yelled. 'Now look what you've done. I nearly had him. We'll never get him back now.'

The following night nobody felt much like going to the disco. We had spent all day being extra quiet, just in case we could hear Persil scratching, but by half past three we were no closer to finding him. The disco was to raise money for a new woodland area at the back of the school, so we had to go, but really we hoped that Mrs Hughes would just cancel it.

'What if Persil is frightened?'

'What if he escapes through one of the outside doors?' We were still pretty sure that he was inside the school somewhere.

'What if he comes out when everybody is dancing and someone squishes him?' Richard had come to collect the register.

Discos in our school are run by the PTA, and my mum and a few others always end up organising things. So me and Alys and Rhodri didn't go home after school. Mum brought us up some sandwiches and sent us to help Mrs Thomas with putting out the cups and saucers in the little room where the science equipment is kept. There's a sink in the corner and that's where they always set up the tea urn. They've got this huge teapot which only comes out for discos and concerts.

When Alys I went to get packets of crisps from the staff room, the teapot was standing ready for action on the worktop. When we came back, it was upside down on the floor and Mrs Thomas was lying on top of it. 'Isabel, get the cage!' she shrieked. 'The hamster's in the teapot!'

Sounds of frantic scratching coming from inside the teapot told me I needed to fetch some extra help.

In the end it took four of us to get Persil back in his cage: one to hold it steady, and another – me – to pick up Persil when Mrs Thomas lifted the edge of the teapot. Richard and Huw stood ready to catch him if he made a run for it. I didn't like the thought of Richard helping, but, by the time everyone else turned up for the disco, Persil was safely back in Hamster Mansions, and Mrs Thomas was being congratulated on her quick thinking.

'How did he end up in the teapot?' Mrs Hughes wanted to know.

'I heard a noise,' said Mrs Thomas, 'and there he was, down by the sink unit. I think he was looking for food. I just crumbled a biscuit into the teapot, put it on its side and in he strolled!'

Chapter 7

Sugar and Salt

After his escape attempt, there were new rules about looking after Persil. My dad said we needed a special run so that if he got out, he couldn't go very far. It became a sort of technology project and we were all supposed to think about it for homework. One morning Steffan raced into class, bubbling with a new and crazy-sounding plan.

'You know where they're putting in the new lights near the chippy?' he said. 'They've got like big Lego, massive red and white cubes all joined together. It's to keep people away from the traffic while they do the pavement.'

We all just stared at him.

Steffan continued. 'They've got blocks like that in Reception. I'll go and ask, shall I?' And before Mrs Thomas could say anything, he was out through the door and on his way down to the infants.

He told us later that Miss Jones, Reception, was a bit surprised when he rushed in and demanded their big plastic blocks, but got really cross when he started helping himself. Mrs Thomas had to go and explain that it was an emergency and we were just borrowing until we could get blocks of our own. Steffan can be a pain, but for once he was a hero, and Mrs Thomas said he would get her nomination for pupil-of-the-week. By lunchtime, he and Helen had set up a run which could be quickly put together and taken apart.

The next few weeks were quite peaceful. Now that Hamster Mansions had its own compound, Mrs Thomas stopped worrying about cage cleaning and we settled back into all the usual Easter term things like the Saint David's Day concert and practising for the first round of the Urdd Eisteddfod. Mrs Hughes had decided that we were going to compete in loads of items this year, so most lunchtimes were taken up with choir practices and rehearsals for the *cyd-adrodd*, the recitation competition. I was in everything and so was Madlen – we hardly got any playtime. Coming up to the first Eisteddfod we were practising all the time. Anyway, when the big day came, we did really well, but instead of making things better, it meant we were through to the next round, where the competition would be even tougher. More rehearsals. Sometimes we even had practices before school.

One good thing – people stopped going straight to Persil's cage every morning and waking him up. Hamsters are supposed to sleep during the day, but poor old Persil got woken up at all the wrong times. Perhaps that's how we didn't know that he had gone missing. It wasn't until playtime, when it was Helen's turn to check on his food and water, that we knew anything was wrong.

On the day of Persil's second disappearance, we were playing tag, all hiding in a big group close to the back door outside our classroom. So everybody saw Helen come streaking across the playground, screaming, 'He's gone! He's gone!'

We all charged.

'What d'you mean he's gone?'

Sometimes people ask the stupidest questions.

I didn't wait for an answer. I didn't care that we aren't allowed into the building without asking the teacher on duty. I didn't care that we aren't supposed to use the back door. I just ran. Everybody ran after me and that is how Mrs Collins found us all in the classroom, in a large group in front of Persil's empty cage.

'Oh!' It was the only thing she said. She could see as well as we could that the roof of Persil's living room was tilted upwards and there was a big gap at the side. That was how he had made his escape.

We looked everywhere – we turned the classroom upside down, but there was no sign of him. After play, a message went round to all classes – infant and junior – and every teacher ordered a thorough search. It was clear that this time Persil had made a much better job of disappearing. School had never been so tidy: every classroom and every cupboard was turned out, the computer area in the library was cleared and even the dressing-up clothes and bit bags were searched and sorted. Nothing.

For the first day or so, every class – even the infants – tried to be really quiet so that they would be able to hear the least little scratch or rustle, but people quickly forgot. Only our class was silent, and that was because we were all so miserable. Even this didn't last very long and gradually things returned to normal. Every now and then someone would think they heard a noise, and everything would stop, but it was just imagination – Persil was well and truly lost.

The weekend came and went and gradually people stopped asking about him. From time to time someone in our class would think they'd seen him, but it would always turn out to be a false alarm. The days turned into weeks and the teachers stepped up the preparations for the next round of the Eisteddfod. We didn't even have proper PE lessons any more, just *dawnsio gwerin* and clog-dancing practice.

In assembly on the Friday before the competition, Mrs Hughes wished us all good luck. She said that we'd worked really hard and it was the taking part, not the winning, that was important. She said she was really proud of us, whatever happened on Saturday.

We were up against some really tough opposition, so I was pleased to come third in the solo singing competition. To everyone's amazement, especially Mr Morris who coaches us, our *cyd-adrodd* party came first. But the dancers were beaten into last place. It was the first year that our school had taken part and it was obvious as soon as the other groups got up to dance that they must have been rehearsing for *years*. Our dancers were just pleased not to have fallen over on stage.

At least now, we thought, we could go back to having proper PE lessons.

From the following Monday, the school hall was back to normal and PE equipment was brought out of its special storage area for the first time in weeks.

It was in the lesson just after morning play, when Gerwyn, who must be the smallest boy in Mr Morris's class, came hammering at our door. He didn't wait for Mrs Thomas to say, '*Dere mewn!*' He burst into the room. 'We've found him!' he said. 'We've found Persil! He's in one of the PE boxes!'

It was true. Our hamster had been found. What Gerwyn didn't tell us was how thin and sick Persil was. Mr Morris immediately sent his class to change, so that they wouldn't all be fussing and crowding around. Mrs Thomas went down to the hall with a shoe-box lined with bedding and, when she came back, she looked very serious. 'Persil's very ill,' she said, 'I don't think he's going to be with us for very much longer.' She put him in a warm place near the radiator and sent me to fetch a dropper bottle from Mrs Collins who looks after the science equipment. 'I don't think he will be able to drink without help, but at least we can give him drops of water to keep his mouth moist.'

When I came back, I was allowed to help with the feeding. Mrs Collins had made up a mixture of sugar water and salt which she said would give Persil a boost of energy. Mrs Thomas knew that I was used to helping with the baby lambs on the farm. When I saw Persil, I nearly cried. He was so thin, I could see his little heart beating, and his snowy fur was all dull and dusty. I put a tiny drop of the mixture onto his whiskers and, at first, it just rolled off, but then his jaw opened just a little and I managed to get some of the liquid inside.

'Not too much,' said Mrs Thomas. 'He hasn't had anything to eat or drink for a very long time by the look of him.'

I found it hard to go back to work and just stared at the multiplication problems on the page in front of me. After a while, Mrs Thomas called me up to her desk and asked if I would like use the punch to put some air holes in the lid of the shoe box. We would have to decide what was going to happen to Persil; he certainly couldn't be left in school overnight, and we would need to put a lid on his box if he was going to travel.

About half way through the afternoon, Richard

came in with a message from Mr Morris to say that late games had been cancelled and people could ring home if they needed to. It was very quiet in our classroom, but even so Richard seemed much quieter than normal and Mrs Thomas asked him if he was feeling all right.

'How's the hamster?' he suddenly blurted.

'Would you like to see him?' Suddenly Mrs Thomas was looking at Richard very sharply.

He just nodded and Mrs Thomas pointed in the direction of the shoe box. We all heard him gasp as he caught his first glimpse of Persil. When he turned to go back to his own classroom, his head was down and he didn't look up even when Mrs Thomas asked him to give the rest of Year Six a progress report.

'He was crying!' Aled was the first to break the silence after the click of the classroom door.

'You don't think,' said Madlen slowly, 'that he had anything to do with Persil getting out of his cage?'

'Well,' said Mrs Thomas, 'that had crossed my mind.'

It had crossed my mind too. It's just the kind of thing Richard would do.

At that moment there was another knock at the

door. This time, it was Madlen's mum with Jonathan. Madi's hand flew to her mouth. She had completely forgotten that she was supposed to be going to the dentist. She quickly got her things together, but instead of rushing to her mum, she hung back and looked over towards Persil's radiator.

'Come on,' said her mum, 'we don't want to be late.'

'We've had a bit of a shock this afternoon.' Mrs Thomas quickly told her what had happened.

By this time Jonathan had got fed up of standing with his mum at the door and had wandered over to Madlen.

'I want to see,' he said.

She took him by the hand and led him over to the shoe box.

Jonathan stared into it for a long time. 'Poor Persil,' he said. 'Come and see, Mum.'

She went over to join them. She was probably worrying what would happen if Jonathan got too close. Madlen was the only person in the class who had had to say 'no' when it was her turn to take the hamster home.

'Oh, poor little thing!' she exclaimed. 'He needs to go to the vet.'

'We could take him, couldn't we, Mum?' Madlen's voice was pleading. 'We could take him on the way to the dentist. I could stay with him.'

'Let's take him now,' said Jonathan. 'Please, Mum.'

She looked at her watch. 'I'm sure Mr Shepherd would understand if we were late,' she said, 'under the circumstances. All right – on condition, Madi, that he stays in the back with you, and Jonathan sits in the front with me.'

I fetched the lid for Persil's box and, within a very short time, we were all wishing Madlen luck as she clutched his temporary home tightly to her chest.

When they had gone, Mrs Thomas told us to pack our things away and we all sat on the carpet to talk about what had happened.

'What if he d-dies?' Stuart said what I guess everybody else was thinking. I certainly was.

'We'll have a funeral.'

It was Steffan's idea. He had decided where Persil would be buried – on the bank behind the infant yard – and he'd even chosen the hymns.

'Oh, shut up, Steff!'

'Yeah. *Cau dy geg.*'

Mrs Thomas hastily told us to put our hands together and close our eyes. We stumbled through our hometime prayer, *Iesu tirion, gwel yn awr,* and then walked miserably down to the hall for the buses. All the other classes wanted to ask questions, but nobody wanted to answer. We had enough questions of our own.

Chapter 8

The Letter

I couldn't wait to find out what had happened at the vet's, but Mum said I shouldn't ring Madlen till after tea. I was terrified that Persil hadn't survived the journey and that she was too upset to phone me. When Mum finally said I could ring, Madi answered at once. At least her voice sounded okay.

'Hi,' she said. 'Don't get your hopes up. The vet says it's touch and go, and it will all depend on the next forty-eight hours. He's given Persil a vitamin injection which seemed to perk him up a bit, and he's given him some special drink – like Mrs Collins made, only better. He's got to have it every couple of hours from a dropper bottle.'

'How are you going to do that? Are you going to stay awake?' I was used to Dad at lambing time, but I didn't think her mum would let Madlen stay up all night.

'We're going to set the alarm and take it in turns. I'll be getting up at five.'

'What about school tomorrow?'

'He'll have to stay here. Mum says she can work at home and keep an eye on him. She's promised to let us know if anything happens.'

'What about Jonathan?'

'Well, that's the really strange thing. He's fine.'

At least something was going well.

The next day in school, everybody crowded around Madlen, wanting to know how Persil was. There hadn't been any change overnight. He had been asleep for a lot of the time, but, towards morning, it had been more difficult to wake him for his feed, and her mum had warned Madi that this could be the beginning of the end. All we could do was wait.

It was a long day, and everybody jumped when the classroom door opened. Madi was allowed to ring home at lunchtime and came back to class saying that Persil was still sleeping. He had been asleep all morning.

In the afternoon we went outside to do a perimeter survey. Our school field is huge and Mrs Collins wanted us to make a list of all the things growing in the hedge. We had a picture checklist of plants and flowers and we had to put

tally marks whenever we found something that looked like one of the pictures. We all had our own little bit to do, and Madi and I worked together.

From across the fields came the sudden 'crack, crack' of a rifle. I looked at Madi. 'Do you think he's all right?' We just couldn't stop thinking about Persil.

When we came back in, there was no new message. Persil was still holding on.

The next morning, Madlen burst into the classroom. She was smiling so it had to be good news. 'Persil's awake!' she said. 'And this morning, he wanted more to drink. Mum's going to try him with some food – she rang the vet, and he said to give him some baby food from the end of a lolly stick.'

From that moment on, the news just got better and better. Every day, Persil was a little bit stronger. Soon he was able to nibble bits of carrot and apple. The main thing now was to fatten him up. Each night, Madi took pictures of him, then brought the camera into school next day for us to see. She printed out the pictures and soon we had a long string of them stretching across the noticeboard. You couldn't see much change from one day to the next, but if you compared pictures a few days apart, the difference was enormous. The day we saw Persil eating from his own food bowl, we knew that it wouldn't be long before he could come back to live in Hamster Mansions, this time with a special security clip on the roof. The cage would need to be spotless. Volunteers washed the chambers and the tower in hot soapy water and polished the sides until they gleamed.

As the day drew closer for Persil's official return, I wondered how Madlen was going to feel when the hamster came back to school. It would feel empty in her house once he had gone. He was going to have one last check-up at the vet's, then her mum would bring him into school on Thursday morning.

It was getting really close to the end of term. In Circle Time we decided that we'd ask Mrs Evans, one of the classroom assistants, to look after Persil over the holidays. Nobody liked the idea of having to take over from Madlen. I know I would have felt really bad if I'd looked after Persil and then had to bring him back to school.

So, on Wednesday morning, I got a bit of surprise when Madi came whizzing into the classroom, threw off her coat and flung it over the back of her chair.

'Guess what!'

I couldn't guess. It could have been anything. You never know with Madlen.

'We've had a letter. It's really cool!'

'Ooh, what?' I couldn't begin to imagine. Had she won some kind of competition? The story – as usual – was long and complicated.

'Mum took Jonathan to the hospital last week, for his check-up at the asthma clinic with Dr Cole, and he told him all about looking after Persil.'

'Yes?' I couldn't see what the hamster had to do with Jonathan's visit to the asthma clinic.

'Well,' said Madlen, 'the doctor was really interested, especially when Mum said his asthma had been fine. He checked the hospital notes to see whether Jonathan had had all the allergy tests.'

'I thought he had those when he was little,' I said.

'Yes,' she said, 'he did, but that was ages ago. Doctor Cole said even though Jonathan might still be allergic to dogs, he could be okay with other animals.'

At that moment, Mrs Thomas came into the classroom and ordered us out to play. 'Coats on!' she said. 'It's a lovely day.'

Out on the yard it was freezing. Little whirlwinds of dust whipped up into our faces and I hugged my duffle coat around me. Madlen didn't seem to notice the biting wind. She just carried straight on with the story.

'So they did some extra tests – there and then – but Jonathan couldn't have the results right away. They had to be checked in the hospital. We got the letter this morning.'

I was beginning to understand. 'What did it

say?'

'Jonathan is definitely allergic to cats and dogs.' Madlen tried hard to keep her voice steady.

'Yes.'

'. . . but he's okay with everything else!' She was fizzing with excitement.

'Does that mean . . ?'

'Yes! Mum's taking us to the garden centre on Saturday! Jonathan wants a hamster, he says, a white one, just like Persil. I don't care. I'll be happy with whatever they've got!'

At that moment, a football bounced at Madlen's feet. She caught it in both hands and wrapped her arms around it. She held it for a moment.

'Hey! Give us the ball back!' yelled Richard.

'Fat chance!' she yelled. 'Fetch!'

She lifted the ball high above her shoulders and hurled it as far away from Richard as she possibly could. And you should have seen the look on Madlen's face . . .

Meet the Author

'Miss, the hamster's out of his cage.'

That was the cry I learned to dread. For some reason the school hamsters belonged to a breed of master escapologists. The only one not to escape was Basil, a tiny grey hamster from Siberia. But he had other tricks up his paw, such as biting anything which came within snatching distance of his cage. He disgraced himself on a weekend visit to Michael Jones by nipping the family dog, a Golden Retriever with a temptingly swishy tail. Basil did not get a second invitation!

Persil, on the other hand, was an amiable chap – who deserved a story all to himself!

Viv